Girlfriend
YOU ARE THE BEST!

❧

a fable for our times

Carol Lynn Pearson

ILLUSTRATED BY
Kathleen Peterson

GIBBS·SMITH
✈P
PUBLISHER

SALT LAKE CITY

For our girlfriends—angels all.
C.L.P. and K.P.

First Edition
04 03 02 01 00   5 4 3 2 1

Text © 2000 Carol Lynn Pearson
Illustrations © 2000 Kathleen Peterson

Published by
Gibbs Smith, Publisher
P.O. Box 667
Layton, Utah 84041

Order toll-free: (1-800) 748-5439
Website: *www.gibbs-smith.com*
E-mail: *info@gibbs-smith.com*

Edited by Suzanne Taylor
Designed and produced by J. Scott Knudsen, Park City, Utah
Printed and bound in China

Library of Congress Cataloging-in-Publication Data
Pearson, Carol Lynn.
   Girlfriend, you are the best!: a fable for our times / by Carol Lynn Pearson;
   illustrated by Kathleen Peterson.
      p. cm.
   ISBN 1-58685-008-3
   1. Female friendship—Fiction. I. Peterson, Kathleen B., 1951–   II. Title.
PS3566.E227 G57   2000
813'.54—dc21   00-026581

here was a girl.
Sweet. Smart.
Lonely.

*S*he loved her teddy bear very much, but the teddy bear did not join the conversation when she talked about hamster houses, the tooth fairy, or how to freak out your mother by turning your eyelids inside out.

*S*he loved her goldfish very much, but the goldfish was quite unsuitable for hugging.

*S*he loved her dog very much, but her dog did not enjoy sharing her clothes or figuring out what went with what.

But one day when the girl opened her mail, there was a card with familiar handwriting that said, "Well, Girlfriend, you are still *very* wrong about *very* many things, but, dang it, you are still the best! Forgive me?"

It took the girl thirty seconds to grab her purse and start the car.

When the girl finished school, she moved far away and got a job and had to get up early in the morning even when it rained and be nice all day to a grumpy boss who told her that her work was not up to speed. Often she was not certain who she was and what she was doing and if her dreams were worth working for.

Eventually the girl met
a man she loved very
much, and she and the
man got married. They
were very happy
together, and the girl felt that she
had found a huge and thrilling
part of who she was. Even so,
sometimes she had more words
than he wanted to hear, and
usually he didn't even notice her
clothes at all.

A thousand angels surrounded her like dancing stars, and the archangel gestured to them with divine pride. "Take a look at *my* girlfriends!" she said. "What would I do without them? Angels, girlfriends—who can tell the difference? Blessed is she that has even *one!* Aren't they the best?"

The girl could hardly speak as she saw a familiar face materialize from a nearby cloud, a face with a smile like the sunrise.

Opening her arms, she managed to whisper—